PUBLISHER'S NOTE

Locomotive is one of those books that sets the standard of book illustration. It was created by the far-sighted Polish duo, Lewitt and Him, in conjunction with the renowned Polish author, Julian Tuwim, in the late 1930s. It was an inspired combination that set the tone for an illustrative partnership that went on to create many remarkable books and saw the two illustrators becoming influential artists and designers, leading the Polish cause in the dark days of the Second World War ("the Lewitt-Him phenomenon," as they were described in 1946). It was just on the eve of that conflict that this book appeared in Polish and subsequently in English and French, at a time when it must have been a shock and a joy to encounter the bright colors and modernist-inflected imagery that tells in visual form the three stories that the book contains. Harking back to precedents in Russian children's book-making and looking forward to the Picture Puffins and other hugely successful models in Britain and North America, it stands out as a beacon of quality and imagination, working its charm for children and parents in the twenty-first century just as much as it did on its first publication eighty years ago.

Roger Thorp

LOCOMOTIVE
THE TURNIP
THE BIRDS' BROADCAST

Rhymes by JULIAN TUWIM *Drawings by* LEWITT AND HIM

Thames & Hudson

CONTENTS

Here is the engine, black, stupendous,

Dripping with oil, its heat tremendous.

Eager it waits; and its body glows,

While the bursts of steam that it pants and blows,

Seem proud, impatient.

CHUFF I'll be off!
UFF I'll be off!
PUFF I will!
UFF I will!

It gobbles up coal with a ravenous roar,
Though it seems too gorged to burn any more.
But soon we are ready: the coaches are fixed,
And also some trucks for goods—all mixed—
Horses, cows, bicycles, umbrellas and chicks.

Look at this trio! Each one a glutton,
Eating sausages of partridge and mutton!

And here is a wagon full  of bananas,

Here is another with  shiny pianos;

In the next  an enormous gun

With blocks of iron to rest it on;

This contains  wardrobes, and tables, too;

And here  are some animals off to a zoo.

Another wagon has lovely fat pigs,
In another are parcels and boxes of figs.
Forty wagons! But I've not been told
What the other thirty hold.

They're all so heavy that a thousand men,
As huge and strong as tall Big Ben,
Each one's weight off the scales,
Could never shift them from the rails.

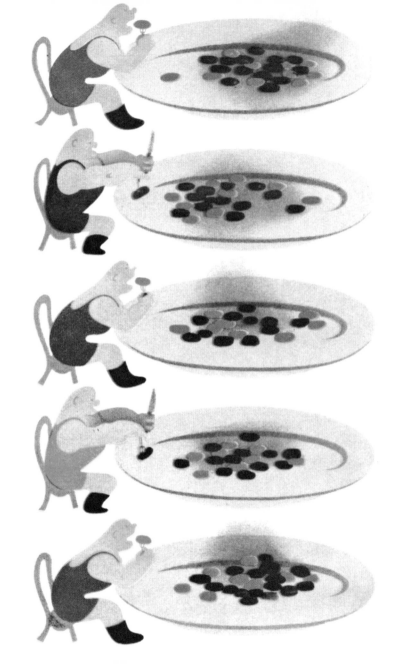

There goes the whistle with its sudden scream,
And now the engine gets up steam
As the wheels turn and the axles creak
With a slow, thin, grinding shriek.
Then bulkily,
      powerfully,
            tugging
                  easily
The train
    starts to move,
          whistling
              breezily.
Crash! as the wagons jerk into motion,
Then rumble slowly out of the station.
But, gathering speed, it starts to race,
And dashes ahead at a furious pace,
With the noise of a hundred singing fountains ...

... by bridges and valleys,

through tunnels   **and mountains,**

It rushes away, for it must not be late,
Into the distance faster than fate.
I've got to arrive in time, in time, I've got to arrive in time!
Easily, smoothly, just like a ball, it rolls downhill, passing us all.
But how does it go? What gives it the power
To go racing along for hour after hour?
First the hot steam from the boiler and fire
Passes through pipes to each valve and piston;
The pressure of steam rises higher and higher,
The wheels whizz round and the train flies on.
Can I mount the slope by the dusty pinewood?
I think I can, I think I can! I thought I could, I thought I could!
Through the fields and cuttings, unseen it tears,
Just as a toy train runs under chairs.
And still the wheels sing with their clashing rhyme,
I've got to be there in time, in time, I've got to be there in time!

THE TURNIP

Grandfather planted a turnip seed,
And the turnip flourished like a weed—
Plump and round and luscious and sweet,
Nice to look at, good to eat.
So Grandpa went out every day
To see if his turnip ought to stay
And go on growing another night—
Till one fine morn it looked just right!
Just right for the pot!
Juicy and hot!
To be put in a stew!
Oo—ooh!

Grandfather thought of the bubbling stew,
So he pulled at it hard—as wouldn't you?
But alas! the turnip would not move.
So "Grandma," he shouted, "come here, my love!
I shall take hold of the turnip top,
You hold me, and we'll soon pull it up."
And they pulled and pulled until they would drop ...

But it budged not an inch. It would have to stay
Till further help should come their way.
Then out ran their grandson, little Theo,
Who saw their fix and took hold of Grannie;
She put her arms round Grandpa again,
And they tugged at the turnip with might and strain.
But they needed more help. Then "Hurrah," cried Theo,
"Here comes my puppy, here comes Leo!"

Then they started all over again:
Leo tugged at Theo,
Theo at Grandma,
Grandma at Grandpa,
Grandpa at the turnip.
But still the turnip stuck in the ground.
So while they rested Leo looked around
To see if further help could be found...
And there was the family cat, called Lady,

Pretending to stalk a hen named Sadie.
So Leo barked, "Lady, come and pull,
We'll have this turnip out of its hole."
So Lady tugged at Leo,
Leo at Theo,
Theo at Grandma,
Grandma at Grandpa,
Grandpa at the turnip.
But still the turnip stuck in the ground,
Though they pulled, and jerked, and grunted, and frowned.

Then Lady called to the little red hen,
"Do come and help!" They got ready again—
And Sadie tugged at Lady,
Lady at Leo,
Leo at Theo,
Theo at Grandma,
Grandma at Grandpa,
Grandpa at the turnip.
But still the turnip stuck in the ground.
And Sadie the hen said, "I'll be crowned
With a comb as large as a turkey's nest

Before I let this turnip rest!
Come here, Sissy, you, you goose,
Let's see if together we get it loose."
So Sissy tugged at Sadie,
Sadie at Lady,
Lady at Leo,
Leo at Theo,
Theo at Grandma,
Grandma at Grandpa,
Grandpa at the turnip.
But still the turnip stuck in the ground.

Yet in for a penny, in for a pound—
So when they saw that long-legged stork,
They asked Chrissy to do some work.
And Chrissy tugged at Sissy,
Sissy at Sadie,
Sadie at Lady,
Lady at Leo,
Leo at Theo,
George at Grandma,
Grandma at Grandpa,
Grandpa at the turnip.
But still the turnip stuck in the ground.

Then suddenly, with a leap and a bound,
As the stork called out, came Philip Frog,
Who hopped to their help from his floating log.

So Philip tugged at Chrissy,
Chrissy at Sissy,
Sissy at Sadie,
Sadie at Lady,
Lady at Leo,
Leo at Theo,
Theo at Grandma,
Grandma at Grandpa,
Grandpa at the turnip,
And Percy the jackdaw joined with Philip—
He liked the look of the juicy turnip.
All the long string of them pulled and craned,
Heaved and jerked and puffed and strained.

A tiring game...
Oh, what a shame!
Till—ooooh, whumpff!!!
Out it came
With a sudden rush!

Oh, what a crush
As they tumbled over
And over and over
And bumped down—flop!
One on top
Of the other!

The turnip sat on Grandpa,
Grandpa on Grandma,
Grandma on Theo,
Theo on Leo,
Leo on Lady,
Lady on Sadie,
Sadie on Sissy,
Sissy on Chrissy,
Chrissy on Philip.
But greedy Percy had the worst fall,
For he was squashed beneath them all!

THE BIRDS' BROADCAST

Hullo, this is the Broadcast from the Birchwood Grove!
A running commentary from the land of the birds,
Who are met together on important matters
And give you the chance to hear their words.
Now, first, to find what is this noise
That rustles the grass at early dawn;
Who shall bathe first in the morning dew
Sparkling upon the summer lawn;
Next, and most important of all,
Where in these woods the echo hides
That reproduces all our songs
Quite incorrectly, and besides
Never pays us a single mite, although we own the copyright.

Before you listen to the meeting
Here is a list of who will be talking;
These are the names of the famous birds
At present chirping, warbling and squawking.

The nightingale, blackbird, the owl, the sparrow,
The cock, the woodpecker, the crow, the swallow,
The robin, the thrush, the titmouse, the bullfinch,
The duck, the goose, and the lovely goldfinch,
The yellowhammer, the quail, and the crested lark,
The golden canary, and the long-legged stork,
Also the brambling and the mischievous starling.

Here is the nightingale! Listen now!
We give the microphone to him. "Hallo!
Hallo allo allo allo
Trilloo trilloo trilloo
Radio adio dio adio
Tralio ralio rilloo trilloo
Radio, hallo, radio,
Hallo, hallo, hallo!"

Now the sparrow! He's interrupting!
"What does this gentleman think he's saying?
Oh, tweet, tweet, tweet! Oh, my word,
I don't understand the bird!

Oh, cheep cheep cheep cheep cheep!
Give me a dictionary! I must look
Into some silly, stuffy book
To understand this song. Do you know,
I believe he thinks that he's Caruso!
Preening his feathers! He's not on the stage!
A disgrace, cheep cheep, an absolute outrage!
Cheep, oh, cheep cheep cheep
Cheep! Chee — eep!"

The sparrow twitters and chatters away
Till up starts the cockerel! What will he say?
He is very angry, swishing his tail,
At this rudeness to the nightingale.

He seems most annoyed. What will he do?
"Cock-cock-cock-a-doodle-doo!"
Up jumps the cuckoo! Now *he's* angry, too!
"Cuckoo cuckoo cuckoo, sir, and who

Are you, you copy-cat, you loafer, you?
How dare you sing my song, cuckoo, cuckoo!
Crow if you like, but don't you cuckoo!
Cuckoo is my song, cuckoo, cuckoo!"

The cuckoo repeats: "Cuckoo, cuckoo!"
The woodpecker answers: "Peck-you, peck-you!"
Now the lapwing is speaking. "Peewit, peewit,
Where have you been? What have you seen?
What are you doing? What are you eating?
Where are you going? Whom are you meeting?"
Now the quail whistles: "Come here, hey!
What have you there? Stop it, I say!"
Now they're all twittering! What a row!
No one can hear what's happening now!
"Let it go!" "Give it to me,
Give it to me!" "Let me see!"
"What have you got? A feather? A crumb?
A twig? A fly? A straw? A worm?"
"I want half, give me half!" "I'll build a nest!"
"Go away, all of it's mine!" "My song is best!"
"No! Yes! Straw! Twig! Best! Worst! Wrong! Right! Wrong! Right!"
Oh, my goodness, now there's a fight!

Here come the police to take them away
And bring to an end the birds' relay!

THE STORY BEHIND THE LOCOMOTIVE

Jan Le Witt and George Him formed the Lewitt-Him partnership in Warsaw in 1933.
They designed advertisements, posters and pamphlets for clients including Galkar
Oil, the Warsaw Post Office, Jabłkowski Brothers and the pharmaceutical industry, as
well as book covers, and illustrations for the literary magazine *Wiadomości Literackie*.

Their work was brought to international attention through publications
such as *Gebrauchsgrafik* and *Arts et Métiers Graphiques*, and in 1937 they
were invited to London by the Victoria & Albert Museum and exhibited
their work at the Lund Humphries Gallery.

The celebrated Polish poet Julian Tuwim was initially asked to write
three poems for children: 'The Bird's Radio', 'The Locomotive' and 'The Turnip'.
The publisher Przeworski connected the three poems into one book under
the title *Lokomotywa*, and commissioned illustrations from Lewitt
and Him. The book was published in Polish in 1938, and in French and
English in 1939, and was immediately a sensational success.

Lewitt and Him are particularly remembered for their World War Two
posters *Shanks' Pony* and *The Vegetabull*, for the Guinness Clock at the
Festival of Britain, and for their many beautiful illustrated books.

Jane Rabagliati (step-daughter of George Him)
Michael Le Witt (son of Jan Le Witt)

Translated from the Polish *Lokomotywa*, *Rzepka* and *Prasie Radio*

Original Polish text © 2006 Fundacja im. Juliana Tuwima i Ireny Tuwim, Warsaw, Poland

English text adapted from the Polish by Bernard Gutteridge and William J. Peace

Publisher's Note © 2017 Thames & Hudson Ltd

'The Story Behind the Locomotive' © 2017 the Estate of Jan Le Witt and the Estate of George Him

Illustrations © 2017 the Estate of Jan Le Witt and the Estate of George Him

First published in English in the UK in 1939 by Minerva Publishing Co. Ltd

This new hardback edition first published in the United States of America in 2017 by Thames & Hudson Inc., 500 Fifth Avenue, New York, New York 10011

Library of Congress Control Number
2017930757

ISBN 978-0-500-65097-4

Printed and bound in China by C & C Offset Printing Co. Ltd